# The Journey of Two Eagles

*The One Who Flew Home
and
The One Who Was Left Behind*

**KAREN MARIE BERNARD-MIÑO**

PROISLE PUBLISHING

© Copyright 2024 by Karen Marie Berard-Miño

ISBN: 978-1-963735-89-5

All rights reserved. No part of this book may be reproduced or transmitted in any form or by any means, electronic or mechanical, including photocopying, recording, or by any information storage and retrieval system, without permission in writing from the copyright owner.

The views expressed in this work are solely those of the author and do not necessarily reflect the views of the publisher, and the publisher disclaims any responsibility for them.

**To order additional copies of this book, contact:**

Proisle Publishing Services LLC
39-67 58th Street, 1st floor
Woodside, NY 11377, USA
Phone: (+1 646-480-0129)
info@proislepublishing.com

# Table of Contents

| | |
|---|---:|
| Comments about this book | I |
| A Journey of Dying and Releasing | 1 |
| My Sweetheart | 9 |
| Future-Tripping | 14 |
| Gratitude for the Cancer | 16 |
| The Madness was Halted | 17 |
| Jimmy's Light | 19 |
| Grieving is Passion | 20 |
| Sadness Overtook Euphoria | 21 |
| A Peaceful Spirit | 22 |
| Peace to My Soul | 23 |
| A Mission | 24 |
| My Mission | 25 |
| More Holiness, Give Me, Oh, Lord | 26 |
| Journey to Find Me | 27 |
| My Precious Children | 28 |
| The Tapestry of Life | 29 |
| Alone with Others | 31 |
| Hugs and Kisses | 33 |

| | |
|---|---|
| ISOLATION | 34 |
| KALEIDOSCOPE OF ANGELS | 35 |
| BE STILL AND LISTEN | 36 |
| CREATING SACRED SPACE WITHIN | 37 |
| JAIME, THE TURTLE | 39 |
| PAIN SHARPER THAN A DIAMOND | 40 |
| EMBRACE LOVE | 41 |
| CONNECTION WITH CREATIVITY | 42 |
| INWARD | 43 |
| EPILOGUE | 47 |

# COMMENTS ABOUT THIS BOOK

**The Journey of Two Eagles** is about my father who died from lung cancer. He loved his family with everything he had and was positive every day of his life. He would say, **"I am OK, honey, I am OK."** It is so hard to move forward in life after the most positive thing in your life moves on to a better place before you and without you. The poems are *inspiring and heart-warming*. I feel for my mom.

-MARY M-E

---

**The Journey of Two Eagles** was a nice short story. I cried, I smiled and I related. The poems are *comforting and spiritual.*

-KAREN P

---

**The Journey of Two Eagles** is a collection *of tender-hearted writings and poetry.* Karen chronicles her journey of great loss, mourning and finally acceptance, healing and grateful joy. She expresses the many faces and stages of mourning with an honest rawness that **truly gives a detailed picture of what it's like to mourn** the loss of a loved one. *Very touching.*

-JULIE B

I cherish this *honest telling* of a family dealing with **a loved one's terminal illness. There is** sorrow, denial, bitterness, tenderness, laughter, hope and love. Ultimately, there is acceptance with the enabling power and spiritual healing offered through the mercy and love of Jesus Christ

-VICK O

---

I really had trouble reading this book because it kept **making me cry. The author's own emotions** shined through her writing making me feel *truly heartfelt* for her.

-PJ G

---

**The Journey of Two Eagles** will *help mend broken hearts and turn them whole again.*

-JAMIE W

---

**The Journey of Two Eagles** is *amazing,* especially of the trials and tribulations of both Jimmy and Karen. It takes a whole lot of love for them both to deal with **Jimmy's illness and their faith in God to overcome the** trials which eventually hones them both to come closer to God. I really enjoyed reading this book and applaud Karen for her strength to overcome her challenges because of her love for Jimmy.

-LOUISE F

This book, **"The Journey of Two Eagles"**, is *truly amazing*. The personal Gethsemane that Karen and Jimmy go through in their lives make you think twice about your own experiences. It *gives you the strength and the will to keep moving forward*. I give really big kudos to Karen for bringing this out in the open. We all need reminding that your time on earth, just like the two eagles, is very special, and makes life worth living.

-MICHELLE T
---

This *poetic diary* of raw human emotions from weeping sorrow to inner peace, clutches at our very **heartstrings. We can feel Karen's pain with every twist** and turn, with every triumph and defeat. Tears well up in our eyes and souls with each turned page. *We can relate*. Our stories may be different but we feel like we have been there. We connect with every ebb and flow of feelings. Hope is left in the wake, validating the uniqueness of our feelings and personhood. *What a journey!* We rejoice as well as cry with her and her family as if it were our own. She definitely brings it HOME.

-SHARON K
---

# A JOURNEY OF DYING AND RELEASING

It all started in 2002 when Jaime ("Jimmy" or "Bubba") went for a doctor's appointment to do a stress test for his heart. I wasn't there.

The results indicated that he needed to go to the hospital immediately but the doctor would not let him drive there by himself. They could not reach me so the doctor took him to the ER herself. Unable to perform an angiogram in that facility, he was taken by ambulance to another hospital in a different city. He failed the angiogram. Now he needed emergency triple bypass surgery for his heart the following day. Oh man, Oh man! I started grief future-tripping. I called all my children. They all rushed to the hospital. Danny, my son, gave Jaime a blessing. In the blessing he was told that he would endure the heart operation. He was also told that he was an example for good and that God was proud of him.

My daughter, Kathy ("Kat"), came up from southern California. Mary, my sister, and her husband came up too. I was scared to my bones. Mary kept us laughing with tales of yesteryears. It helped to keep the mood lighter because we were all so scared. The doctor had to use the skinny veins in his legs to correct his heart. It was an eight-hour surgery. It was pretty rough for the doctor. In the recovery room, it was not good. We all went home because they told us to. I did not feel good about this decision. I got the feeling something was happening so we all went back. Kathy was beside herself. She did not believe me when I said I had this feeling about Daddy, so she called the nurse who was taking care of him. Sure enough, something had happened to his heart. They gave him medicine to help his heart pump because it was weak and failing. *Take a deep breath,* I told myself. When things get scary, I tend to hold my breath.

We were all worried. We went back to the hospital, a long drive for so early in the morning. Kathy and I went into his room. Seeing him in an unresponsive state, Kat cried out, "Daddy, Daddy, don't leave! Stay here! I need you!" I believe Jimmy came back because he heard her anguished plea. Then a couple of hours later we went back in and he was awake. Alleluia! He was going to make it.

We all could breathe again and laugh and talk. Each child was allowed to go in the room and talk to their daddy. However, this started the roller coaster ride of our lives. Hang on tight! It is going to be scary and twisty. He was determined to get better. One step at a time and one day at a time. He did get better from sheer faith in God and his own positive attitude about life. He wanted to be here and that is the short of it.

It was simple to him. He lived in the present. What was so hard about that? He couldn't figure out why I always lived in the future. It actually annoyed him. "I am not dead yet," he would say to me. He treated every day as a gift from God with such positive gratitude. I made him a shirt that said "GO GO GO". He was Mr. Energizer. Never say it is the end. Keep going was his slogan. He kept going and going at all odds. He lived! We walked around the hospital floor arm in arm with slow steps. He complained about the dirty toilet so I cleaned it for him. It was a disgusting *puke mess. It was disgraceful for a hospital to be so dirty. My poor husband only liked to go potty at home, so this was absolutely horrifying for him. We could hardly wait to get him out of this filthy hospital before he got a staph infection. Early on the third day, he was discharged but the doctor sent him home too early. He ended up the same day back at the hospital but at another one closer to our home. What a difference! He stayed there three days and got better.

One year later, another surgery was in order. He had a blocked carotid artery in his neck so the doctor put a stent in it. He still could work at this time. He recovered nicely. But a few months later he was coughing up blood. I took him to the ER. The kids took him to another hospital for a CAT scan. I met them there later because of work. After the tests were done, we were told it was lung cancer, and he needed to start radiation and chemo immediately. Our hearts sunk to the floor.

A year later, he was coughing up blood again. Back to ER. My tears rolled down my cheeks furiously. The dam broke in our tear ducts. We embraced each other Of course, Dad's positive attitude reigned again. "Stop crying," he would say. "I am not dead yet! I am going to live twenty more years."

He never complained. He lived in the present each day. As I prepared my heart for him to die, he lived for today, happy. I kept future-tripping. It was so frustrating. I buried him so many times. Each time he made me out a liar. I was so grateful for this. I missed so much life because of my fears of tomorrow. No matter how awful the diagnosis, he remained calm and content. He remained humorous and calm throughout radiation and chemotherapy.

Not me. I had to talk to everyone. I had to help him holistically. I searched and searched the web for cancer cures. I came upon blood-stabilizing supplements that can be used throughout chemotherapy. The pills kept his red and white blood cells intact and plentiful so he had infrequent blood transfusions compared to others receiving chemo. The doctors were amazed. His blood cells were not destroyed. I felt good helping him.

When our daughter, Mary Patricia, found out that her dad had cancer, she went on a hunt for alternative cures too. She helped me a lot, searching and searching until we found a good diet and supplements to help him stay on the earth longer. He wanted to stay as long as he could to see his children and grandchildren.

One more baby being born. "Oh goodie," he would say. "Let's go see him/her." He loved holding the babies no matter how weak he was. We never missed a birthday party or holiday get-together. His family was everything to him.

Then he got pneumonia. Oh, man! Coughing, more coughing up blood. It looked like pieces of his lungs falling out. These were the most challenging years of our lives, from 2005 through 2007. He was in and out of the hospital. I thought I was going to lose him when these episodes occurred. My fear crept up every time. I would hold my breath and plead with God, "Not yet!" I needed my poor husband who was so very sick. He was my sanity, my stability, my anchor, my soulmate, and my love.

I needed to talk to someone. I needed answers. I needed help with my emotions of him dying. It hurt. My heart would ache so much that I thought I was having a heart attack. The roller coaster ride was getting fast and furious, scary and twisty. He'd say, "I am going to live!" and I would say, "You have cancer!" I stopped talking about his death sentence with him because I didn't want him to think that I had given up. He was so positive.

How could I be negative? I was resting in realism. I kept future-tripping about his death. I started to prepare individual little boxes for his ashes. I also made some for myself so he would not become anxious about his own death. I prepared a memorial, his celebration of life. I went to the crematorium and got that in order. There would be little to do when he actually died. I prepared for the worst and hoped for the best. Another day with Jimmy, I would say. Together we received group and individual counseling through the hospital, hospice, and community outreach. It eased my pain and I was so grateful that he supported me throughout my grief. He was fine, but anything to oblige "Mama" was his motto.

Jimmy received many blessings. He was told in these blessings that God extended his life here and that he would not suffer any pain. He would recover for a while. Then he would get worse again and be very weak. I couldn't live in the present until the day the doctor prescribed Tarceva. That oral drug cost $3,600 a month. Medicare and supplemental medical insurance paid for it.

We were so blessed in 2008. Jimmy's cancer shrunk into little lesions so we had a magnificent two years without hospital visits. He went on hospice for a little while but he didn't stay on it long. He was determined to be healed. By December 2008 there was hardly any cancer left. What a miracle!!! This is when I learned to live in the present.

In 2008, I can't remember which month, I sent him to Ecuador with Kathy while he was feeling good. He had to have oxygen because of the altitude. It was a sacrifice for me to let him go. We didn't have enough money for me to go so Kathy went. The other children could not go because of their obligations with their families. Besides, Kathy is a nurse. I felt comfortable letting him go with her in case she was needed for his health. As it turned out, one night she felt impressed to check on him. He was not breathing. She shook him and put his oxygen back on him. It was a good visit. I am glad he had this time with his family.

Jimmy would say that he was "OK" no matter how he felt. I still went to cancer support groups. It helped me a lot to hear about other people's Victories. It gave me hope.

Plus, it helped me to talk it through – my feelings, and how we were coping with this death sentence. At least that is what it felt like to me.

I loved being near him. We didn't say much. It didn't matter. I just loved his sweet spirit. I could kiss and touch him. No matter what, he did the dishes. He made breakfast and dinner until Sunday before he died. *SOB! SOB! SOB!* He was an attentive and cheerful husband until the end.

One of the best times we had was when we took a trip down to southern California. We stopped at every temple on the way. San Diego was our most favorite temple. Jimmy understood the sealing blessings for the first time because the sealer spoke in Spanish. Jimmy is from Quito, Ecuador. His native language is Spanish. It was so nice to hold his hand and be so close to him in the temple. Our love is forever and we shall be with each other again. Alleluia! Thank you, Jesus, for your gospel.

In October 2009, I sent him down to Kathy's for a month. I did this for both of them because I knew he was dying. I wanted him to go while he was still well. It was hard to be without him but I knew he would be back, unlike death, when he doesn't come back. *SOB! SOB! SOB!* I felt he needed to visit Kathy because she lived so far away and it was hard for her to take time off work. This way she could see him every day even while she was working.

I appreciate all the help my children gave me while Daddy was so sick. My daughter, Karen ("KK"), would often take us to the hospital because she lived so close to us and I was so distraught.

In December 2009, he started to get sick. He had pneumonia. An x-ray also revealed that the cancer came back with a fury.

On March 1, 2010, hospice was brought back on board. Chaplain Paul was so soothing for us. I was beside myself. He asked me if I could put Jimmy in the palm of my hand like a baby bird. Then when he is ready to go, I can let him go. That was the day, March 24, 2010, I wrote the following poem for him. I could never share this poem with him. I didn't want him to know that I knew it wasn't long before he would be here no longer.

# MY SWEETHEART
## A PRAYER
**March 24, 2010**

My Sweetheart! I hold you like a bird
As your wings are broken
I try to mend them
You lay still in my hand
I pet you and comfort you
I embrace you and feed you,
my eagle companion

Go home. Fly to Father
He awaits your arrival
Oh, your family is preparing
a beautiful mansion for you
They are planning a great reunion
There will be laughing, hugging and dancing
I wish that I could see
and be a part of the great homecoming

As I hold you in my heart
I lay you at the feet of Jesus
He will pick you up and say
"Well done, my special brother"
He will heal every wound
and you will fly with your family eagles

I love and adore you
Fly home, Honey, fly home
Be at peace

JIMMY FLEW HOME MAY 12, 2010

Jimmy, my sweet Jimmy, just the right person for this talented hyper, extremely emotional lady. He took me as I am, never desiring to change me. He just accepted me with all my ups and downs. When I look back, how unstable I was! That makes him a saint.

The month before he died, he finally knew that he was leaving. We embraced each other and wept holding each other so tight. One week before he died, he held my hand the whole time while we watched TV. That never happened in 37 years despite my requests. It was a tiny miracle. Wouldn't you know it, he left this world after he finally responded to the longing of my heart. Man, I felt cheated. I couldn't do the hand-holding dance anymore.

The week he died, Kathy came home for a few days. It was Mother's Day weekend. On Sunday, May 9th, KK with her sons, Jordyn ("Jordie") and Robert Jr., came over and fixed us breakfast. It was a hash brown casserole. Oh, yummy! It was fabulous! That night Kat bought us Chinese dinner. This was our favorite food. Jaime especially liked fried rice with sweet and sour pork. My daughter, Jamie, along with Mary Patricia and Dan came over to pay their respects to their dad. I was glad to see all of my children. On Monday, May 10th, Jimmy made breakfast for us. He was a super good cook. He loved making eggs with rice. Oh, yum! I don't know how he had strength but he did it anyway. Then things started to turn around for the worst. Not all at once but step by step. Kathy thought he was okay so she decided to return home. She felt comfortable to leave. When she left he could walk with a walker. A few hours later he could sit in a wheelchair. A few hours later he was at the commode to go to the bathroom. Then a few hours later the urinal was all he could use. He never got out of bed again.

Something told me to have him call his sisters in Ecuador. They had a good visit. I am sure they were crying. I felt he needed to say good-bye. Did he? No, of course not. *"I am OK,"* he would say. He ate his last meal, leftover Chinese sweet and sour pork with fried rice, his favorite meal. He never urinated or ate again. I called Kathy that night and told her that her dad was not doing well. She couldn't believe it but she came the next day anyway. I am so grateful to Mary Patricia for picking her up at the airport on Tuesday night. I could not leave his side. He was dying.

Tuesday, May 11th, KK, Jamie, Dan and Mary Patricia came back. Mary was beside herself. "Daddy, Daddy, please wake up," she pleaded. No one wanted to believe that he was dying but he was. He would slip into a coma coming up once in a while. Jamie just kept busy by cleaning our home and then taking a wet washcloth and wiping his brow and kissing him on his forehead. How tender she was! I was so grateful for all her hard work and quietness. KK and Dan were very quiet too.

The pastor and the nurse from hospice also came on Tuesday. Jimmy came up out of his coma to greet them.

"Are you OK?" the pastor asked.

"Oh, yes," was his reply. Then he went back under. Then he came back up again saying, "I had a dream." We never found out about his dream because he went back under never to come up again.

Mary Patricia returned in the late evening and dropped Kathy and Jordyn off. They slept over in case I needed their help while I kept vigil. I could not sleep. He was dying.

On Wednesday, May 12, 2010, at 8:45am Jimmy passed. Oh, sooooooo hard! Kathy laid next to him for an hour. The other children arrived and said their goodbyes. Then the elders from my church came and changed him into his temple clothes. He looked so peaceful. He had such a beautiful smile on his face. When the morticians came to get him, I asked them if I could have fifteen minutes alone with him. They said, "Okay."

My children were waiting outside. I can't even know their pain except when I lost my father, it was like losing a part of me. Grief is so painful and felt in so many different ways.

Now I had to finalize his memorial. I had most of it done. We held it on Saturday, May 15th. KK was really helpful in decorating the chapel. Kathy and Dan gave their thoughts about their dad. I ranted on about my sweetheart. Jordie had to come up and get me. I could not stop talking. Then the children and grandchildren sang, "I Am a Child of God". It was so touching. I was so grateful to my whole family. My sister, Sharen, came for the memorial. She helped me a lot after the service. I collapsed when it was over. I had not slept in three days. My blood pressure was extremely high. An ambulance was called. When I was stabilized in the ER, she took me home and stayed with me. I needed so much rest.

Now we all have to move on without my beautiful husband and companion, their father and grandfather. I miss him so much. I call out to him ever so often to see if he is listening. I am sure he is and protecting me too. I am so proud of Mary Patricia. Through all her grief, she planned her wedding without her daddy. K was her right arm. All the girls stuck together and made it such a beautiful wedding. Jamie and her precious girls looked so adorable. The handsome men in our lives were simply awesome.

The hardest thing to do was to walk down the aisle with Mary Patricia arm in arm, me holding Jimmy's photo but I did it at her request. Danny stepped up in Jimmy's place and danced the first dance with her. It was so nice to see. I cried and laughed, laughed and cried all night long. Mary was married on May 30, 2010 — 18 days after her precious daddy lost his battle with cancer and returned to his heavenly home.

Life is sure different without him. I kept myself busy with gardening at the Kaleidoscope garden. There people grow and donate fresh food for hospice patients and their families. It filled my time with something I love to do. Besides, it gave me a chance to give back what they gave us while Jimmy was sick. God answered my prayers to join such an organization for my healing. I was so blessed to be among such beautiful people.

# FUTURE-TRIPPING
## August 17, 2010

Oh-oops-he is dying
Oh-yes-he is recovering
Oh-no-oops-he is dying again
Oh-yes-he is recovering

Man—back and forth, forth and back
Is there no end to this madness?
I am living 20 years more, he'd say
Taking a deep breath, I would say OK

I knew the inevitable
He had lung cancer, emphysema and heart disease
My-oh my-20 years, is that possible?
Inside, I would cry and cry.

Oh-no-not again dying
Oh-man-yes-yay-recovering
Oh-no-not again ER
Oh-yes-yay-he is BETTER

One breath at a time
One day at a time, Karen
Live in the present
Jimmy is living there

Worried, so worried
Jimmy would ask,
"Do you have enough for today?"

"Yes," would be the reply
Then, no need to worry for today

Future-tripping causes pain,
pain unbearable and hopelessness
Where are the hugs and kisses for today?
Where are these precious moments of embrace?

Future-tripping was not his game
How many days did I lose?
Tripping on his ill health
when he would say everything is fine

Future-tripping became invisible
when he was free for 2 years
We lived in the moment
All was better. We were grateful for today

# GRATITUDE FOR THE CANCER
**August 17, 2010**

Cancer taught me love

Cancer taught me forgiveness

Cancer taught me to live

Cancer taught me the present

Cancer taught me gratitude

Cancer taught me life

Cancer taught me patience

Cancer taught me slowness

Cancer taught me humility

Cancer taught me love

# THE MADNESS WAS HALTED
**August 17, 2010**

The madness halted on May 12, 2010
It came to a screeching halt
No more bloody tissues
No more ER trips
No more barely breathing
No more laughing
No more crying
No more kissing
No more pulling out teeth
No more hand-holding
No more slow walking
Just the silence of movement
Could I have this madness back?

If I could only have him back,
to touch, to hold
to laugh with, to cry with
to make love to, to kiss
to watch TV with, to shower with
to embrace, to wiggle our toes with
to dance with, to move with
Yes, the madness has halted

Now the emptiness has appeared
Another madness, loneliness
has appeared upon the scene of life
Oh, just for a little madness of Jimmy
would be worth all the gold in the world
The quietness overcomes my soul

The depth of solitude is forbidding
And yet, life must go on for me now
Without the madness of my honey's last moments
Jimmy, if you are listening,
"Help me!" with the madness of solitude

# JIMMY'S LIGHT
**August 17, 2010**

Jimmy's light shines in my world
He watches me day and night
I hear his prayers for me
A little off course I travel
Jimmy's light brings me home
Jimmy's light surrounds our children
Jimmy's light is felt by our grandchildren
Jimmy's light is like unto Jesus'
Jimmy's light fills the room with love
Jimmy's light beckons to me
Jimmy's light holds me
Jimmy's light forgives me
Jimmy's light is glorious
Jimmy's light is eternal
Jimmy's light surrounds me
Jimmy's light is peaceful
Jimmy's light is harmonious
Jimrny's light teaches me
Jimmy's light is gratefulness
Jimmy's light is God's light
Jimmy's light shines in our world
AMEN

## GRIEVING IS PASSION
**August 17, 2010**

Oh, my soul is in pain for my beloved
Come back, I cry---I miss you
I want to touch you again
Please come back, my sweetness
My soul cries in despair
To continue life without you
How can I go on?
Just what does life hold for me?
Without you---I don't know where to begin

Comfort my soul, Oh, Lord
The grief is so passionate
It consumes my every being
It washes my body with my tears
Laughter helps my soul heal
so grief can be less passionate
Then it will disperse
because healing has overcome
the passion of grief

Through the laughter of appreciation
grief is exchanged for gratitude
Now my pain is lifted
to new heights of understanding
God has sent angels to surround me,
to comfort and laugh with me
Grief is losing its passion
Though I miss my beloved,
my soul releases the pain of separation

# SADNESS OVERTOOK EUPHORIA

**August 17, 2010**

Then one week later
sadness started taking over
That did not feel well
A lump in my throat
A twinge in my heart
A feeling of brokenness
crept in day by day
I couldn't kiss my love
I couldn't touch his tender body
I couldn't squeeze his hands
I couldn't touch his soft skin
I couldn't dance with him anymore
I couldn't smell his aroma,
the aroma of magnetism
I couldn't smell his stinky feet
Hmmm---Taking a deep breath
No, can't smell him anymore
Yes, sadness overtook euphoria

# A PEACEFUL SPIRIT
## August 18, 2010

On the journey home
he whispered, "I had a dream…"
He illuminated so much peace
A dream… Can we know your dream?

When he came up to visit
a smile of peace radiated his face
And when he took his last breath
a smile of peace remained

# PEACE TO MY SOUL
## August 17, 2010

Peace, oh, peace to my soul
The gospel comforts me
assuring me, I will see him again

My precious love lives
He lives, my precious love lives
Peace overtakes the tears

Quietness of mind rests on the day
Oh, peace to my soul
for knowledge of eternal life

One day, we will meet again
embracing in our love for each other
Oh, peace to my soul, he lives

# A MISSION
**August 17, 2010**

A Mission to fulfill
so he was called home
Working with his family
Sharing the everlasting gospel

A Mission to fulfill
to teach others how to love
Teaching them slowness of anger
Teaching them about grateful hearts
Teaching them the miracle of Jesus

A Mission to fulfill
so he was called home
to embrace his friends and family,
to teach them Christ's pure love

Jimmy, go and fulfill your Mission
Your wife bids you adieu
Go forth and teach others to love
like you loved me
and how you loved your family
and most of all, how you loved God

## MY MISSION
**August 17, 2010**

I, too, was called on a Mission,

a Mission to lift burdened souls,

to wipe away the tears of yesteryears

I have been called on a Mission

to bring laughter to aching hearts,

to bring joy to little ones,

to strengthen the weak,

to comfort those who mourn

Laughter, a gift given to me by God

to bring a smile to anyone

willing to receive it

Karen, go and fulfill your Mission

# MORE HOLINESS, GIVE ME, OH, LORD
**August 17, 2010**

More holiness, give me, Oh, Lord

Holiness — trampled by a fragile mind

Holiness — given up for worldly frolic

Holiness — tempered by repentance

Holiness — given back to me by God

Holiness — my soul reaches for

Holiness — my core thirsts for

Holiness — to be more like God

Holiness is a grateful heart

Holiness is a sacred thought

Holiness is caring for every living thing

Holiness is stopping to say hello

Holiness is walking with another

Holiness is creating life

Holiness is caring for yourself

Holiness is respecting all God's creatures

More holiness, give me, Oh, Lord

# JOURNEY TO FIND ME
## August 18, 2010

How do I find me without Jimmy?
Walking alone is emptiness unfolding
Who am I? This Karen of grace
How do I walk beside another?
How do I walk with myself?
How do I dance with the nurturing me?
Be quiet and listen to your heart
You love the Lord and you love people
You love your precious sons and daughters,
all images of your beloved
Twirl in and out of their lives
You make a difference with your smile
Your laughter brings joy to their souls
Who are you, my friend, Karen?
You are a woman of grace
You are a woman of intelligence
You are a woman of beauty
You are a woman of God
You are a woman of gentleness
You are a woman of kindness
You, my friend, are whole within
Walk alone and love you
You are worth loving you
You twirl and dance and leap for joy
You, Karen, already have found you
You are a poet, a woman of many words,
the words of life for yourself and others
Karen, you are a gift of living
You are a blessing to all you meet
The journey to find you is here

# MY PRECIOUS CHILDREN
**August 18, 2010**

In the faces of all my children
I see my beloved
So, at times, it is hard to stay
Emotions of loss become reality

Tears swell up in my heart
Then they roll down my cheeks
and yet, I think… If I stay
I can relish the laughter
and noises of the living

I see my beloved in all my children
He dances, swims, laughs and plays
If only I would listen
I could bear him through
the beings he left behind

How rich I am!
Money can't buy
all my beautiful children
clothed in the glory of their father
touched by the twinkle of eternity

How blessed we all are
to have each other
The grief seems distant
as I watch my children
Plus the joy of our grandchildren
reigns in my heart
Our richness is our posterity
AMEN

# THE TAPESTRY OF LIFE
**August 18, 2010**

Walking through a garden
Smelling the rose which just opened
Filling my senses with its fragrance
puts a smile upon my face


Watching a child hug a dog
Watching a child splash in puddles
Watching a child chase the birds
puts a smile upon my face


Twirling and dancing to the rhythm of my own song
Crocheting and talking while riding on a bus
Laughing and giggling with my new playmates
puts a smile upon my face


Planting and watering the flower of today
Nourishing and pruning their essence
Watching them bloom into loveliness
puts a smile upon my face

Thinking and thanking God
Running and stretching my whole being
Laughing in gratitude for today
puts a smile upon my face

Giving a dollar or two to a man without means
Sharing time with another
Writing a new verse
puts a smile upon my face

Weaving the tapestry of life
Linking little motions together
Making new sounds of harmony
brings smiles to many faces

# ALONE WITH OTHERS
**August 20, 2010**

So many people and yet alone
A feeling of oneness
Where is my sweetheart to whisper to,
to kiss on his cheek and hold his tiny hand?
Alone and yet, so many people
How to exist alone?


One moment at a time
breathing and smiling at strange faces
Will somebody come and walk with me,
chat and listen to me?


I need you, someone
The loneliness is unbearable
"GOD!" I cry out,
"What do you want me to do?"


Just smile inside, be you
The person who matches you
will soon appear so life isn't empty anymore

He will come and you will know I have
prepared him to meet you
You are worthy of him

Now be comforted, my daughter
Be at peace, know I am aware of thee
My hand stretches forth to you
Feel my arms around you

1 will comfort and give you peace
Your heart will be full of laughter
Soon the pain of loneliness will leave
Another will walk by your side
Now you know how to treat another

This is why you need time alone,
to see your worth and the worth of another
So you are alone with so many people
It is OK. Breathe and smile and listen

# HUGS AND KISSES
**August 20, 2010**

When you wake up, give a hug
When you leave, give a kiss
I would hear as I walked out the door

Go back and give him a kiss
Oh, if I only could give him one more kiss
Only if I could engulf him in my bosom

Oh, my sweet Jimmy, I love you
Feel my kisses and feel my hug
Hugs and kisses are only memories

Now I can give them to my children
Oh, give me a hug as I greet a grandchild
Hugs and kisses, kisses and hugs

To those who mean so much to me
I won't withdraw my affection
I will give lots of hugs and kisses,
kisses and hugs

# ISOLATION
**August 20, 2010**

Do I choose isolation?

Sometimes. I want to be alone

sitting just far enough away

to listen to the chitter chatter

And yet, I am alone. I choose it this way

Meditative. I don't want to respond

If I just sit a little ways away

I can hear the laughter and the silliness of life

I can fill my heart, anyway

Though I choose isolation

I must understand, I choose this

choice of mine, I don't really know why

It's OK, just go within

Maybe it will change this feeling of isolation

In an instant I might choose to be a part of the whole

This very minute, I choose isolation

# KALEIDOSCOPE OF ANGELS
**September 11, 2010**

Press on, Karen, to make the quilt of life,

colors to blend in harmony,

giving and sharing the joys of eternal life

For all life is eternal beginning to end

Friends whispering hope to ones in pain

Cooking angels, bringing food to

unburden the suffering

Caretakers of the garden, bringing joy and life

Oh, the Teddy Bears of hope, bringing smiles to faces

Children anticipating the toys of shared blessings

God building the foundation of hope, love, and mercy

Thank you, God, for all your kaleidoscope angels

pressing on to make the quilt of life

# BE STILL AND LISTEN
**September 11, 2010**

Be Still in your sacred space
Listen to your heart beat
Listen to the birds chirping
Listen to the fragrance of mums growing
Listen to the breath of life
Listen to a baby crying into mortality
Listen to the peaceful rhythm of one dying

Listen to the harmony of people praying
Listen to your knees creaking
Listen to children laughing
Listen to the sound of music playing
Listen to the quiet sounds of rocks being
Listen to the waves crashing upon the shore

Listen to the cars buzzing by
Listen to the quiet small voice of the Spirit whispering
Listen to inspiration
Listen to the sound of hymns playing in your heart
Be Still and Listen, oh, my soul, to
the tunes of God's creation

# CREATING SACRED SPACE WITHIN
**September 11, 2010**

God says, Go inside. Listen to my voice
Remove the clutter of life and just be
Breathe in life's creations
Dispel all the tensions of havoc
Simplify thy life to the I AM
Then you shall understand ME,
the giver of life eternal

Smell the glorious aroma of life
Flowers blooming, ribs barbequing, bacon frying
Enjoy the scent of a clean kitchen
Smell the fragrance of bathing in peppermint
Incense burning in a chapel refreshing the soul
Aromatic gasoline filling the car
Smell, oh, smell the fragrance of new life

Now taste the elegance of music
creating a space for worship and meditation
Bring objects of tenderness
to taste the sweetness of life
Taste the bitterness of loneliness
Now taste the spirit of giving to others
Taste the luscious ripe tomatoes
Taste the beauty of the attending gardener

Now, my child, enjoy the sacredness of solitude
I will be there in your thoughts
Quiet yourself to hear my voice
I will call out to thee to do my work
Be still, my child, and create sacredness in thy soul
Dispel the anxious world of disharmony
Then inside of you the peace, love and joy will begin

# JAIME, THE TURTLE
**September 11, 2010**

Jaime radiated the slowness of the Land Turtle

and the swiftness of a Sea Turtle

His thoughts were methodical,

not twisting left or right,

trusting God to help him through life's challenges

Steady as he goes, firm and vivacious

His shoulders carried the weight of many men

and yet, his stature stood straight

He cracked a sweet smile when he was happy

The steadiness of the Turtle was in his eyes

# PAIN SHARPER THAN A DIAMOND
**September 12, 2010**

Today the pain could cut through glass like a diamond

It is so sharp, the longing for him to hold me

Tears rolling down my cheek

making my eyes sore with prickles

My mouth opens with wet screams

longing to hold my sweetheart

Oh, when will this pain cease to be so alive?

He whispers, It is going to be OK, Honey

I answer, For you, you are there and I am here

I ask, Is the pain of separation as hard for you as me?

He says, It is different but I miss holding you.

I ask, When can I come home?

He answers, When your work is finished

Bring laughter to all who will receive it

It is your gift to soften all the pain

I answer, Please help me do that

He says, I am always with you

Nevertheless, the pain is sharp as a diamond

# EMBRACE LOVE
## September 22, 2010

Jesus says love your God
He also says love yourself
Then He says love your neighbor
Then he says love your enemies

Embrace the light of all mankind
Walk in love and faith
Have no fear of differences

God loves all His children
Shall we do less than God?
I don't think that is wise
Just embrace love to all mankind

Put your arms around each other
Embrace your differences
God is the author of love
He teaches His children to do the same

Our commandment from God is to love
If we do this, we will see a change in the world
Peace, love and harmony will abide
for all eternity and this present life

# CONNECTION WITH CREATIVITY
**December 2, 2011**

Oh, creation — God within

Paint a picture — Write a poem

What makes you glow within?

The water rushing on the shore?

Birds squawking and scampering on the beach?

People laughing for sheer laughing?

Laughing, smiling, painting, writing, and dancing

are all your gifts of creating happiness

Breathing in the fresh air of the beach

consumes my soul's desire,

motivates me to write and paint

When will you pack and move

to the place of your heart's destiny?

The waves are calling me home

Rejoice in life, they seem to say

COME BE WITH US AND CONNECT

AMEN

# INWARD
**December 2, 2011**

Time to turn inward
to the core of my soul
Feed the hungry, laugh with the hurting

Peace and harmony abide
When I turn inward
to ponder the gifts I have to share

God has blessed me with friends
God has blessed me with laughter
God has blessed me with wholeness

Go in peace, my child
I hear in a soft voice
whispering in the crashing waves

Listen to the stories that people tell
Feel their love and devotion to life
Then you will walk with grace

As you grow inward
where love abides in your heart,
your spirit will dance and twirl

For you, my daughter
now you are on the light path
to bless yourself and others

Victory, I hear my soul say
Freedom to be ME

Alleluias reign inside of me, shouting
I AM FREE TO BE ME
Rejoice in the inward garden
of beautiful thoughts and magical gifts

These gifts are ready to sprout out
to give life to a soul in mourning
Now I see the rays of the sun

Reaching inward to bless my life
the light radiates from within
to bless all who meet me

Blessed is the time to reflect
inward gathering of thoughts and gifts
to share with the loneliness of the world

# EPILOGUE

As I have gathered my feelings and thoughts about life without Jimmy, I have grown immensely. Am I the same woman as before he left? No, is the answer. I have come unto myself. I am more understanding of my own needs. I am fully alive with the knowledge that I can ask for what I need.

I walk in this life to give service to myself, family and friends, and others who seek my help. Most of all, I am in the service of my Lord and Savior. Without him, I would be a lost sheep. Now I am cradled in His care. He carries me when I can't do it anymore. Oh, my beloved Savior, thank you for helping me through this difficult time. Now there is a new beginning with another man who loves the Lord. He is such a help to me. He also adores my children and grandchildren, and honors my late husband. I love him so much because of his tender mercy towards me. Thank you, God, for sending this man to me when I was so broken. He loved me anyway and still does. Jan, thanks for being you and loving God as I do. Life is simple and sweet.

## THE JOURNEY OF TWO EAGLES

The One Who Flew Home

And

The One Who Was left Behind

This book was written for the purpose of healing
from Karen and Jaime's journey with cancer
and his eventual death. These poems depict
the anguish of a broken heart and
the roller coaster ride of cancer.
It is also a victory story over grief.

Karen Marie Berard Miño was born in Spokane, Washington in 1947. She is the oldest of six children. She grew up in a faith-building family who loved Jesus.

Jaime Efren Miño was born in Quito, Ecuador in 1935. He was the youngest of ten children. He came to the United States in his early twenties to live with his brother Jorge.

Jaime and Karen met in a restaurant where they were a cook and waitress in Walnut Creek, California. They were destined to meet. One day Karen asked Jaime to go to the San Francisco Zoo with her two boys and her. He said yes.

*"So we went and had a beautiful time."*

At the end of the day, Karen and Jaime sat on a blanket while the boys played on the swings. Then out of the blue Jaime asked Karen to marry him. To his surprise, she said yes.

Karen and Jaime were married on January 27, 1973. They have four beautiful daughters. Karen and Jaime worked hard, especially Jaime. He worked six days a week just to support his family. Jaime also supported Karen on her journey of healing from abuse. It was not easy for them because Karen was so broken raising six children and trying to keep her sanity. He supported her when she needed to get away and get help for her disturbed mental anguish.

The journey continued in peace and harmony. They hardly ever fought. They just loved each other through the rough times and happy times. His eyes always adored Karen. She is so grateful for the special unconditional love he had for her.

*"We loved to go dancing often embracing each other and twirling one another on the floor."*

Then one solemn day they got the news of his fatal cancer of his lungs. They were devastated, especially Karen. She was going to lose her precious Jimmy of thirty-seven years. With tears in their eyes they went on a journey of recovery, they hoped. The doctors gave him one year to live. They said no way. With Jaime's faith and Karen's organic diet and the doctor's chemo treatments and oral pills, he lived eight more years just to hold one more grandbaby.

He died on May 10, 2010,

Karen felt so alone. She was alone for the first time in her life. 62 years always having someone to be with and take care of and then nothing. She was beside herself. She went to a support group called Kaleidoscope. It helped some. Then she was made master gardener of their organic garden to help cancer patients. Digging in the garden helped her heal some. Then she went on an adventure to Harbin Hot Springs. There she met many beautiful people. There she was introduced to Laughter Yoga. She thought, *'well I haven't laughed in eight years let's go find out what that was about.'* Laughing for no reason. It was great. Her soul started to lighten up. She loved it so much she became a Laughter Yoga Instructor. It has been a blessing to her ever since.

After two years of healing, in 2012, she married Jan Dekruif. He was an answered prayer. He has helped Karen fill the hole of loneliness due to Jaime's death.

Along with Karen and her family, he participates and lovingly supports them in gatherings that celebrate Jaime's life and legacy.

She now serves at a homeless mission in Ukiah, California. She prayed for many days about how she could serve the homeless. The answer was The New Hope Mission. She makes soup once a week and does Laughter Yoga. It helps Karen serve God in a safe environment. She feels so blessed. Her life is rich and full.

Karen and Jaime now have nineteen grand children and seven great grand children.

Karen's belief that families can be forever sustains her joy to be reunited with Jaime. She gives thanks to God every day for her journey in life whether it be challenging or easy she praises God for every blessing.

If you have questions or require further details, you may personally contact the author at:

   karenberardmino1@yahoo.com

www.ingramcontent.com/pod-product-compliance
Lightning Source LLC
LaVergne TN
LVHW050026080526
838202LV00069B/6939